Life in Pictures
Pink Floyd

Marie Clayton

Trans
Atlantic
Press

Forming a band

Pink Floyd pictured in the mid-1960s, from left: Nick Mason, Richard Wright, Roger Waters and Syd Barrett.

In 1962, Roger Waters left Cambridge for London to study architecture at Regent Street Polytechnic. There Waters became interested in music and invested in an acoustic guitar. Eventually he shared a house with Nick Mason and Richard Wright, who were on the same college course, and the three of them joined a band formed by fellow students Clive Metcalf and Keith Noble. In 1964 Syd Barrett (born Roger Keith Barrett), also arrived in London, to study at Camberwell School of Art, and he soon hooked up with his childhood friend Roger Waters.

Barrett, Waters, Mason and Klose, another Cambridge musician, formed a new band, and since their landlord Mike Leonard – a lecturer at the college they all attended – was a keen musician he was sometimes invited to join in. The line-up had Syd Barrett on rhythm guitar, Roger Waters on bass guitar, Nick Mason on drums, Bob Klose on guitar and Mike Leonard on keyboards. At first the new band was named Leonard's Lodgers, but later briefly became The Spectrum Five and then The Tea Set. Richard Wright, meanwhile, had dropped out of college and headed off for an extended holiday abroad before starting a new course at the Royal College of Music.

Both the name and the line-up of the band changed a few times but early in 1965, Barrett had taken over as the main vocalist and at around the same time Richard Wright returned to the UK and was quickly drafted in to replace Mike Leonard on keyboards.

During 1965 the band was sometimes billed as Pink Floyd and sometimes as The Tea Set. By the beginning of 1966 it had finally settled on the name Pink Floyd.

A stable line-up

Roger Waters pictured in 1966. Bob Klose quit the band in mid-1965, leaving a final line-up of Syd Barrett on rhythm guitar and vocals, Roger Waters on bass guitar and vocals, Nick Mason on drums and Richard Wright on keyboards, saxophone and vocals. At first the band's set list mainly consisted of rhythm and blues material from established artists such as Bo Diddley, Muddy Waters and Chuck Berry – like many other fledgling bands at the time – but they soon began to include more original material written by Syd Barrett. After Bob Klose left the band and Syd became front man, the direction changed to include more improvised and original music, with classical influences introduced by Richard Wright.

Coloured and moving lighting effects soon became an essential part of Pink Floyd's stage show.

Light and sound

Pink Floyd on stage at the Roundhouse, Chalk Farm, London, on October 15, 1966. The band had performed at a "psychodilia" music event staged at Hornsey College of Art in November 1966, and students at the college had designed a light show for the evening under the auspices of the band's old landlord, Mike Leonard, who was also a lecturer at Hornsey. Leonard had been developing a "light and sound" system in which the light effects were controlled by the sound, first using recorded and then live music. The use of coloured and moving lighting effects soon became an essential part of Pink Floyd's stage show, and one of the trademark features of their performance.

Under new management

It was a series of repeat performances at The Marquee Club in London during the first half of 1966 that really began to move Pink Floyd forward. These gigs were not so much concerts as performance events – albeit on a small scale – and although they were not widely advertised they found a key audience through word-of-mouth, and at one of these budding pop group manager Peter Jenner heard Pink Floyd play. Jenner realized that this new band could be the more mainstream group he was looking for but his initial approach was rebuffed since the band members were all still full-time students and not sure if they were planning to continue playing, but when he approached them again later that year they agreed that he could represent them.

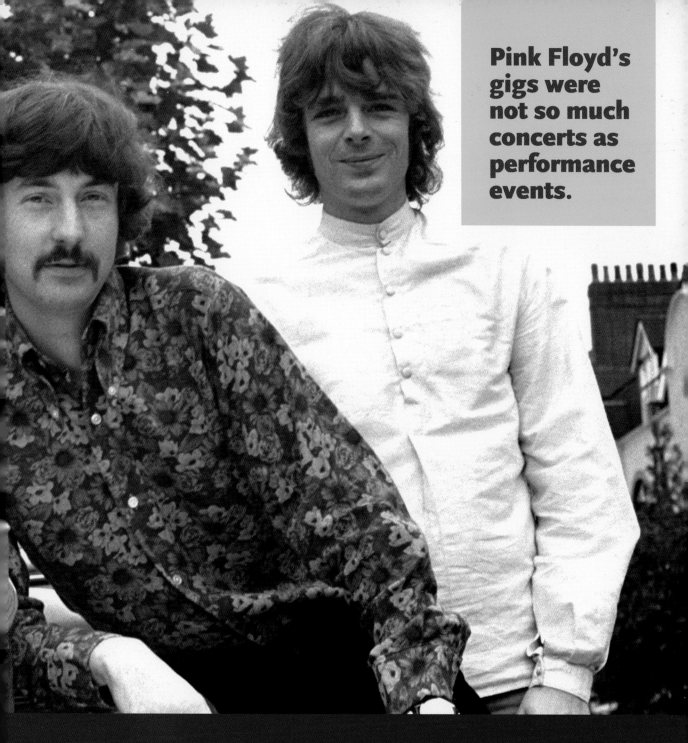

Pink Floyd's gigs were not so much concerts as performance events.

Having signed up Pink Floyd, Jenner brought in Andrew King, who was in charge of booking gigs and also provided funding for new amplifiers. The company, called Blackhill Enterprises, had some success at booking the band for a series of concerts at small venues, and later that year forged a partnership with up-and-coming booking experts the Bryan Morrison Agency, who had established contacts with national venues. Pink Floyd had begun to receive good coverage in the music press and soon began work on a demo tape to secure a recording deal, as well as recording soundtrack music for a documentary, *Tonite Let's All Make Love In London*, funded by the British Film Institute.

In February 1967 Pink Floyd were signed to EMI. The four band members gave up their studies for good and turned professional.

Record deal

Jenner's former partner, John Hopkins, had introduced the band to Americans Joel and Toni Brown, who created lighting effects using slide projections to enhance their act. Such effects had become common in America but caused a sensation in London, and news of these new and exciting performances spread like wildfire. Meanwhile Pink Floyd's demo tape was played to several major record companies, and by February 1 they were signed to EMI. Although the deal did not offer much money, it did allow them considerable creative freedom.

First single

The band had recorded "Arnold Layne" – written by Syd Barrett – in January 1967 as part of their demo tape, since it was a traditional pop song with catchy lyrics. EMI selected it to be the first single and had planned to re-record it in their own studio with their producer, but in the event it was the original demo recording that was released. The lyrics told the story of a transvestite who stole women's underwear from washing lines – which led some radio stations to refuse to play it, although it received plenty of airtime from the BBC. There was even a short film of the band on Wittering beach to promote the single, and they were recorded for BBC's *Top of the Pops*, although the segment was never broadcast. The single reached the UK Top 20, but did not make it any further up the charts.

OPPOSITE AND BELOW: Rehearsing for their first concept show, Games For May, at the Queen Elizabeth Hall in London, on May 12, 1967.

Games for May

Richard Wright, Syd Barrett and Roger Waters check out the timpani during rehearsals for Games For May. The show featured an early experiment with quadrophonic sound, with additional speakers placed at the back of the hall to create a primitive "surround-sound" effect, controlled by a joystick that could direct the sound from any point. It also had the by-now trademark light-and-film display augmented by bubble machines, while during certain sections real flowers were tossed into the audience. Promoter Christopher Hunt had previously specialized in classical music, but he took a risk with Pink Floyd and this concert became a turning point in their career, firmly removing them from the underground music scene and into the mainstream.

Waters in rehearsal. Reviews of *Games For May* were generally positive: the *International Times* hailed it as "a genuine 20th century chamber music concert", while the *Financial Times* called it "the noisiest and prettiest display ever seen on the South Bank". Unfortunately the bubbles and the flower petals stained the seat upholstery and carpet, and Pink Floyd were banned from ever playing the venue again. Worse still, the prototype sound-control system – designed by Bernard Speight, an engineer in EMI's Abbey Road Studios, and dubbed the Azimuth Coordinator – was stolen after the show. Several new compositions were written for the show, including "Games For May", which became the basis for the next single, "See Emily Play". "See Emily Play" was released just after Games For May and did significantly better in the charts than the group's first attempt. As a result, in July they appeared on BBC television's *Top of the Pops* and were featured for three weeks in a row.

"a genuine 20th century chamber music concert"

Piper at the Gates

ABOVE AND OPPOSITE: Pink Floyd pictured outside EMI House (above left to right: Nick Mason, Rick Wright, Syd Barrett and Roger Waters). The band's first album, *The Piper At The Gates Of Dawn*, was released in August 1967. Unusually for the period the deal with EMI had included the development of an album, although the contemporary market was mostly for singles. Although EMI were convinced that Pink Floyd were good, their music was very unlike that of other groups and so a decision had been taken to allow them as much creative freedom as possible and see what ensued. The title of the LP came from the name of a chapter of the book *The Wind in the Willows*, by Kenneth Grahame, and the tracks included a mixture of songs and instrumentals. It was received very positively on release, and although it only reached No.6 in the UK albums chart it went on to be regarded as one of the seminal psychedelic albums of the sixties.

Recording of *Piper at the Gates of Dawn* began at Abbey Road Studios early in 1967 but they returned to Sound Techniques Studio to work on 'See Emily Play'.

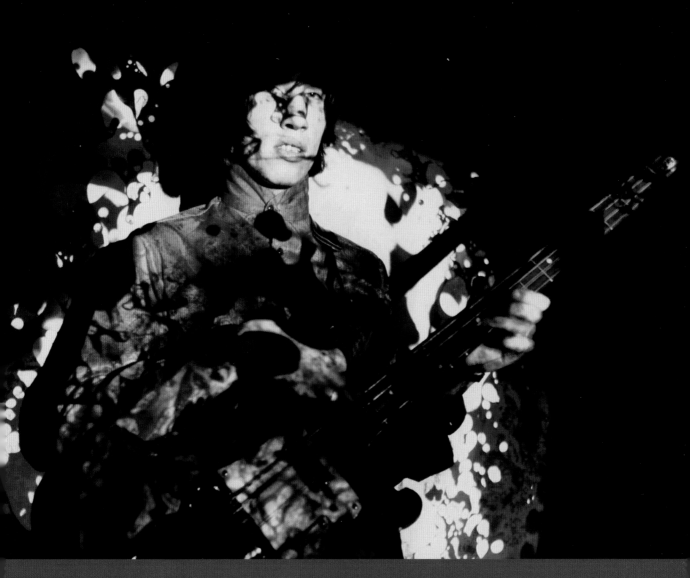

Psychedelic effects

Photographer Andrew Whittuck took a series of atmospheric pictures of the band using their light show. The concept of psychedelic lighting effects was brought into question during the first half of 1967, after the British weekly *News of the World* claimed that they were intended to illustrate the effect of hallucinogenic drugs, and that Pink Floyd's music celebrated drug abuse. EMI quickly issued a statement denying that the music had any connection to drugs and Pink Floyd themselves went on record to state that to them the term "psychedelic" meant the use of sound and light as part of their performance and was not meant to promote the use of LSD or any other drug.

Although Pink Floyd had found an audience in London, outside the capital many of those coming to concerts expected to hear music similar to the band's singles, and were usually outraged to be presented instead with a wave of indeterminate noise played at very high volume and long instrumentals. It wasn't long before promoters began to insist that the band would at least play their released songs as part of their set – although Pink Floyd never gave up on their determination to introduce more avant-garde material.

> "Apples and Oranges" was the last Barrett composition to be released as a Pink Floyd single.

In the recording studio

ABOVE: Roger Waters, Nick Mason, Syd Barrett and Richard Wright at a mixing desk in the recording studio control room. Although they had not played any concerts in August the band had not neglected their recording commitments, spending time in the studio putting together tracks for their planned next album. In October they returned to the studio for more sessions, and to record the next single, "Apples and Oranges". The first album had mainly been filled with Barrett compositions, but he had provided very little new material for this new one and so both Roger Waters and Richard Wright stepped into the breach to come up with a selection of tracks between them. "Apples and Oranges" was the last Barrett composition to be released as a Pink Floyd single, but it did not do as well in the charts as their previous singles.

A troubled state of mind

Syd Barrett at the keyboard. Although he was a supremely talented songwriter and a charismatic personality, Syd didn't have the extrovert nature required for being constantly in the limelight and found the pressure very difficult to handle. Most members of Pink Floyd had nothing to do with drugs during this period, but Syd had begun to experiment heavily with LSD and instead of helping him relax it often brought on bouts of severe stage fright. From mid-1967 onwards his behaviour became increasingly unpredictable and this soon began to cause problems in Pink Floyd's professional life. At some performances he would just stand still, not playing or singing. In an attempt to resolve the situation, that August Pink Floyd's managers Blackhill announced that Syd was suffering from nervous exhaustion and cancelled all concerts for the rest of the month.

Waters began to take over as the spokesman for the band, since Syd was sometimes not in a fit state to be interviewed.

The end of the beginning

ABOVE: Pink Floyd in Copenhagen during their first overseas tour in September 1967. The concerts in Denmark were followed by the band's first US tour, which had originally been timed to coincide with the release of their first album there at the end of October. However, problems with visas meant that the first few dates had to be cancelled. On top of this, the band's celebrated light show did not look at all spectacular in the massive American venues, although the slide projections were still acceptable. And apart from the technical problems, it was on this tour that Syd Barrett really began to fall apart, sometimes standing stock-still without playing or detuning his guitar until the strings fell off during concerts, and refusing to answer questions when interviewed. It wasn't long before Pink Floyd were packed off back to the UK, with several important gigs cancelled.

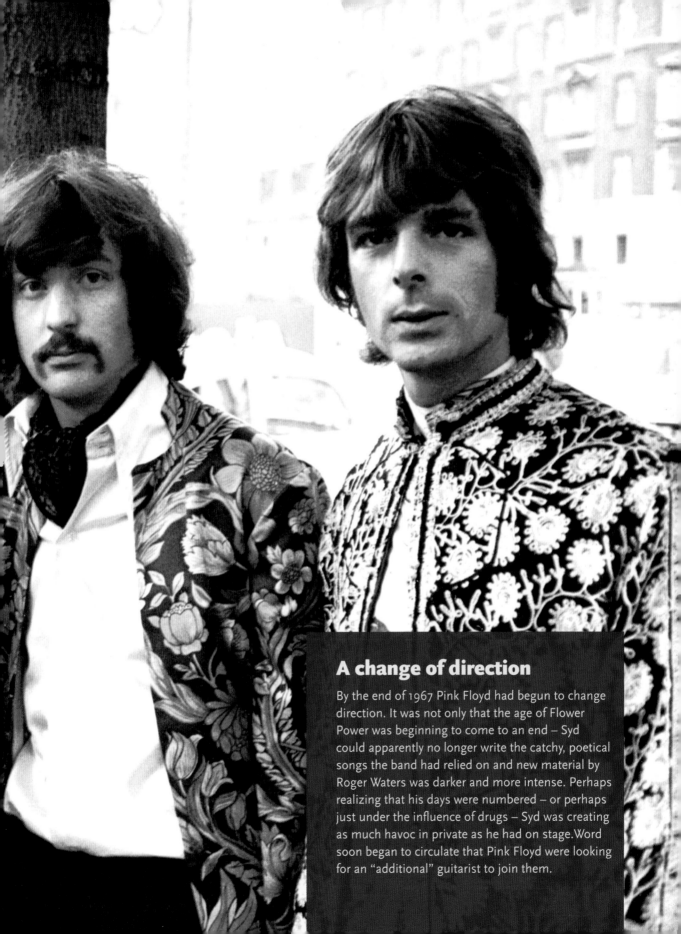

A change of direction

By the end of 1967 Pink Floyd had begun to change
direction. It was not only that the age of Flower
Power was beginning to come to an end – Syd
could apparently no longer write the catchy, poetical
songs the band had relied on and new material by
Roger Waters was darker and more intense. Perhaps
realizing that his days were numbered – or perhaps
just under the influence of drugs – Syd was creating
as much havoc in private as he had on stage. Word
soon began to circulate that Pink Floyd were looking
for an "additional" guitarist to join them.

A new line-up

The new Pink Floyd – from left to right Nick Mason, David Gilmour, Roger Waters, with Richard Wright at the front. The original plan was to have a guitarist on hand who could cover for Syd when he was not functioning, and would otherwise act as a back-up player. The ideal person seemed to be David Gilmour, who had been a friend of Syd's back in Cambridge and who was a talented guitarist. He learned Syd's vocal and guitar parts, but almost immediately it became apparent that the plan was not going to work. The five-man Pink Floyd played a few concerts in January 1969, but Syd did less and less each time until finally the others just didn't bother to pick him up one day on the way to a gig. David Gilmour said later that he found it difficult to take his place as a full member of the band at first, partly because of the shadow of Syd over all of them, and partly because there was no clear idea of the role he should be playing. Although he was undoubtedly talented, his natural style was very different from Syd's and so it was not just a question of stepping straight into empty shoes.

The next album, *A Saucerful of Secrets*, released in June 1968, was a reflection of this time of flux – it had no real sense of direction, except that it had moved away from psychedelia. Despite this, it was quite well received.

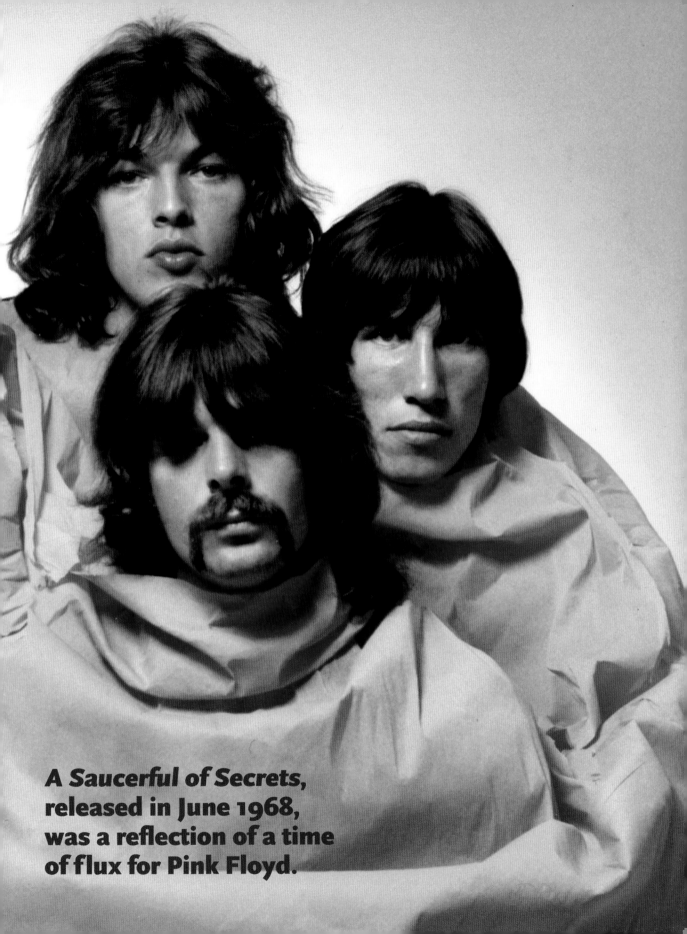

**A Saucerful of Secrets,
released in June 1968,
was a reflection of a time
of flux for Pink Floyd.**

Conquering Europe and the USA

David Gilmour on guitar in 1968. During 1968 Pink Floyd undertook a couple of short tours round Europe and another short tour of North America that brought excellent reviews in the press and a fervent crowd of new fans. In June they headlined the first free concert in Hyde Park – an ideal opportunity to re-launch the band in the UK and unveil the new direction their music was taking. The following year they consolidated their position in the UK with a spectacular event at the Royal Festival Hall that featured the new Azimuth Coordinator, a 360° surround-sound system, and the music arranged to tell a story so the performance became more theatrical event than concert. 1969 also saw Pink Floyd embarking on their first proper national tour of the UK, culminating in a stupendous concert at the Royal Albert Hall in London. They also recorded the soundtrack for the movie *More*, and released their own new album, *Ummagumma*, but perhaps the highlight of the year was an invitation to compose the music for the BBC's coverage of the Apollo 11 moon landing, which was broadcast to millions of viewers and brought the band amazing publicity.

Atom Heart Mother

BELOW: Mason pictured in 1970. In between their concert commitme[nts]
had gone back to the studio to develop an instrumental piece that v[...]
basis of the next album, *Atom Heart Mother*. The new instrumental
and a choir and took up the whole of one side of the album. On the
member was featured in an individual track. "If" was written and su[...]
"Summer '68" was written and performed by Richard Wright, "Fat C[...]
and performed by David Gilmour, and "Alan's Psychedelic Breakfast
in three parts divided by dialogue and sound effects of one of the ro[...]
breakfast in Nick Mason's kitchen, had sound effects created mainly
in later years both Waters and Gilmour were very critical of *Atom He[...]
was released it brought the band their first No.1, in the UK Album Ch[...]

Two new albums

After the success of *Atom Heart Mother*, the pressure was on to come up with another hit album as soon as possible. However, the band had tight touring schedules already in place so would not be able to spend a great deal of time in the recording studio for some time. As a temporary solution, EMI decided to put together a collection of songs from the early years – including "Arnold Layne" and "See Emily Play", from when Syd Barrett was with the band – that had either only been released as singles before, or been included on an album in a shorter version. It also included one previously unreleased track, "Biding My Time", by Roger Waters. This new album, entitled *Relics – A collection of Bizarre Antiques and Curios*, was a budget release so was not eligible for inclusion in the album charts, but it sold well and kept the eager fans happy until the band could come up with some new material. Meanwhile the band had begun work on a new project: taking many unconnected bits of music, using ideas from previous sessions and working the whole lot together into a cohesive whole. This became a piece known as "Return of the Son of Nothing", which was later renamed "Echoes" and used as the entire first side of the next album, *Meddle*.

Atom Heart Mother Live

The music festival at Bath in Somerset was a three-day event, the forerunner to Glastonbury, and it was here that Pink Floyd unveiled "Atom Heart Mother" officially for the first time, with a live orchestra and choir on stage. The festival, which featured some of the world's best groups, had an audience of around 150,000 and Pink Floyd did not come onto the stage until very early on Sunday morning when most festival-goers had been up all night. However, their spectacular performance woke everyone up. The piece was peformed again the following day in Rotterdam but this time they managed without the live orchestra.

In 1971 the band undertook their most extensive North American tour to date as well as playing dates in Japan and Australia but the highlight of the year was a collaboration with French film director Adrian Maben, who filmed them performing against the dramatic backdrop of the ancient Roman amphitheatre at Pompeii. The film also included the first performance of "Speak To Me", which was to become the opening sequence of the next album, *Dark Side of the Moon*.

OPPOSITE: Pink Floyd pictured in Hamburg and (below) in Copenhagen.

The Dark Side of the Moon

Roger Waters had started writing lyrics for the new work at the end of 1971, and in the first few weeks of 1972 the band began rehearsing before taking the entire work on tour. They had often previewed individual pieces in concert before recording them, but this time they played the entire work, in the order it would later appear on the album, which gave them the opportunity to adjust and refine parts that needed improvement. It was at the first concert on a UK tour, at the Brighton Dome on January 20, 1972, that *The Dark Side of the Moon* was to be played for the first time in its entirety but unfortunately technical problems led to only part being covered before the band moved on to other material. It was finally fully presented in mid-February, to immediate acclaim from both the musical and the national press. Throughout 1972, in the US in April and May and then in Europe later in the year, they featured *The Dark Side of the Moon* during the first half of almost all their concerts but played the more established material in the second half.

The band were also invited to write the soundtrack for a movie titled *La Vallée* in 1972. The album was released in June as *Obscured by Clouds*.

Waters came up with the concept of basing pieces around the theme of things that drove people mad: conflict, greed, the pressures of fame and success, the strains of touring, fear of flying ... and mental breakdown.

A new confidence

Waters on stage in 1972. Writing all the lyrics for *The Dark Side of the Moon* and managing to create a complete piece of work on one theme had given Roger Waters a new confidence in his abilities, and it was around this period that be began to consider himself as the main creative and driving force of Pink Floyd. However, there was as yet no sign of the disagreements that would ultimately tear the band apart.

Superstar status

Richard Wright, David Gilmour, Nick Mason, Roger Waters in England, 1973. Much of the first half of 1973 was taken up with a major US tour to coincide with the release of *The Dark Side of the Moon* album. It was all a far cry from the early days when Pink Floyd would arrive in a single van; now the tour equipment took up two 40-foot articulated trucks and the band travelled with their own stage hands, soundmen, electricians, lighting men and other technicians. The stage setting took nearly a full day to assemble at the venue. *The Dark Side of the Moon* is frequently ranked as one of the greatest rock albums of all time and its incredible success quickly propelled Pink Floyd to superstar status. The phenomenal selling power of the album brought the members of the band considerable wealth for the first time and it was also at this time that their collaboration as a group was at its peak.

The song "Money" from *The Dark Side of the Moon* was released as a single in May 1973 and became the first Pink Floyd single to make it into the top twenty on the *Billboard* Hot 100 chart. The music and lyrics were both written by Roger Waters, but the instrumental jam section was a group effort, with David Gilmour contributing guitar and vocals and Richard Wright and Nick Mason improvising their parts.

The Dark Side of the Moon was released in March 1973. It went straight to No.1 in the US *Billboard* 200 chart, had been certified Gold within less than a year and went on to become one of the best-selling albums of all time.

Touring The Dark Side of the Moon

At the end of 1973 the band decided they could afford to take some time off and there were no more concerts between November 4 and June 18 1974, when a tour of France began. Some dates were cancelled when the venues realized they could not cope with the massive power requirements of the band's equipment, or did not have the ceiling height to accommodate the huge 40-foot circular back projection screen that now formed the backdrop to the stage set.

In the winter the band toured the UK and, as usual, the concerts were used to preview and adjust some of the songs intended for the new album: "Shine On You Crazy Diamond", "Raving and Drooling" and "Gotta Be Crazy". The second half of the concert covered *The Dark Side of the Moon*, featuring stunning and innovative specially commissioned animation by Ian Eames. Although the UK tour was a complete success with every venue sold out, some parts of the music press had begun to turn against Pink Floyd. In particular, young reviewer Nick Kent had been very dismissive of the band's new material in an article in *New Musical Express*. However, touring commitments meant further recording of the new album had to be put back to 1975 and fitted in between two US tours, so there was plenty of time to develop the material.

The large circular screen made its appearance in 1974; it went on to become a trademark feature of the band's shows for some time.

Wish You Were Here

With the 1974 winter tour over, the band had a short break over Christmas and the New Year before they were scheduled to begin recording again for the next album, *Wish You Were Here*. Recording sessions were held at EMI's Abbey Road Studios from January 6 to March 3, 1975, but at the end the album was still nowhere near completed. By this time it had been nearly two years since Pink Floyd had released a new album – *A Nice Pair* was simply a re-release of the first two albums – and the record companies were pushing for something to sell. Sensing an opportunity, the band's old company, Capitol Records, released a compilation album, *Tour '75*, to satisfy the fans and build sales of the back catalogue that they still owned.

During one of Pink Floyd's recording sessions, Syd Barrett turned up at the studio to watch. None of the band recognized their former friend at first: he had put on quite a lot of weight, and had shaved off all his head hair, including his eyebrows. After suffering from diabetes for some time, he later developed pancreatic cancer and died at home in Cambridge in July 2006.

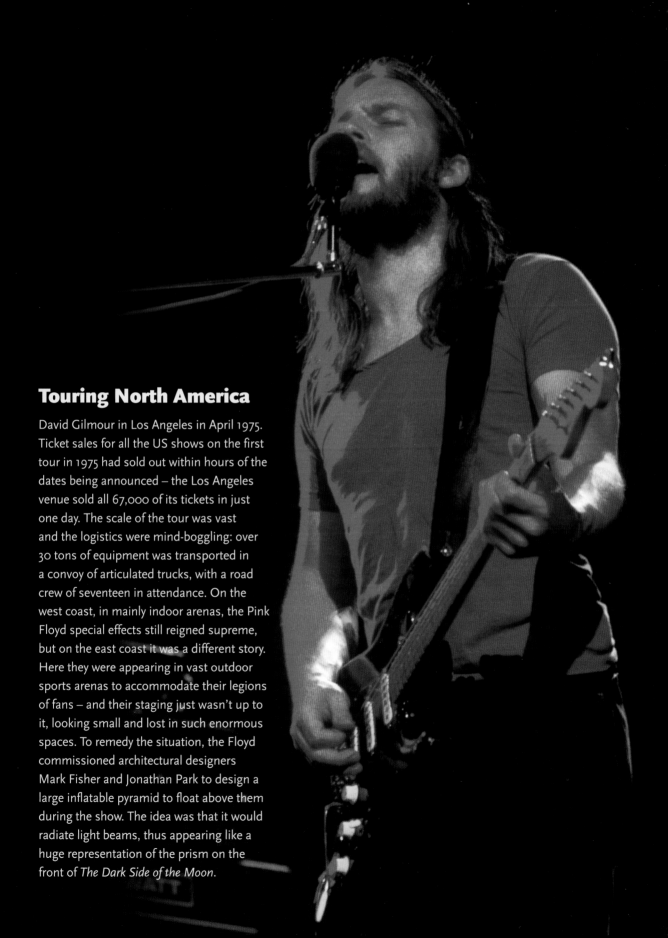

Touring North America

David Gilmour in Los Angeles in April 1975. Ticket sales for all the US shows on the first tour in 1975 had sold out within hours of the dates being announced – the Los Angeles venue sold all 67,000 of its tickets in just one day. The scale of the tour was vast and the logistics were mind-boggling: over 30 tons of equipment was transported in a convoy of articulated trucks, with a road crew of seventeen in attendance. On the west coast, in mainly indoor arenas, the Pink Floyd special effects still reigned supreme, but on the east coast it was a different story. Here they were appearing in vast outdoor sports arenas to accommodate their legions of fans – and their staging just wasn't up to it, looking small and lost in such enormous spaces. To remedy the situation, the Floyd commissioned architectural designers Mark Fisher and Jonathan Park to design a large inflatable pyramid to float above them during the show. The idea was that it would radiate light beams, thus appearing like a huge representation of the prism on the front of *The Dark Side of the Moon*.

Richard Wright in LA. *Wish You Were Here* was eventually released in September 1975. Despite the problems during its creation, both Roger Waters and David Gilmour have said that it is their favourite Pink Floyd album. It went straight to No.1 in the UK chart and reached the top spot in the US a week later, and has continued to sell well over the years: it was certified six times platinum (6 million copies sold) in May 1997.

Waters in particular was upset by playing large venues and he finished the In the Flesh tour stressed and exhausted.

Animals

During 1976, Pink Floyd concentrated on their next album, *Animals*. It has been said that it was during this process that Roger Waters began to assert his domination over the others and pursue his own agenda, gradually trying to turn Pink Floyd into more of a vehicle for his personal vision than a creative collaboration as it had been in the past. Waters' concept for *Animals* was to illustrate the human condition – which he felt was generally suffering from moral and social decay.

The Animals, or In the Flesh, tour began in West Germany two days after the album was released and was built around performing both *Animals* and *Wish You Were Here*. During "Pigs" a giant inflatable pig was supposed to float around the stage above Pink Floyd and the show also featured other inflatables: a giant mother, father and children on a sofa, and later also a car and television set. These were the band's answer to playing vast open venues, bringing the spectacle alive even for those far away at the back. Part of the concert also featured an animated film by Gerald Scarfe that was projected on a big screen behind the band, and showed gory effects such as a city flooded with a sea of blood and a decaying head.

Recording The Wall

Gilmour, Wright and Mason all worked on solo projects in the late '70s but following significant losses on investments the band returned to the studio in 1979 to work on a new album based on an idea suggested by Waters entitled *Bricks In The Wall*. The scale of the concept required a double album and Waters also planned a tour and a film to go with it. The storyline covered events in the life of a rock star—loosely based on Waters himself—including the death of his father at an early age, an overprotective mother, unpleasant experiences at school, the break-up of his marriage, and the downsides of being on tour. Each of the unpleasant experiences becomes a brick in a wall, which eventually separates the star from his audience. Eventually the star manages to pull the wall down, but the end of the album leads back to the beginning.

   It was during the recording of *The Wall* that Pink Floyd's method of collaborating began to fall apart. Roger Waters felt a strong sense of ownership of the material and Gilmour had strong ideas of his own that he was determined to get across. Nick Mason was close to Waters but had developed other interests outside Pink Floyd, while Richard Wright was suffering personal problems and was frequently distracted. There was tension between the four band members and producer Bob Ezrin often had to act as a mediator between Waters and the others.

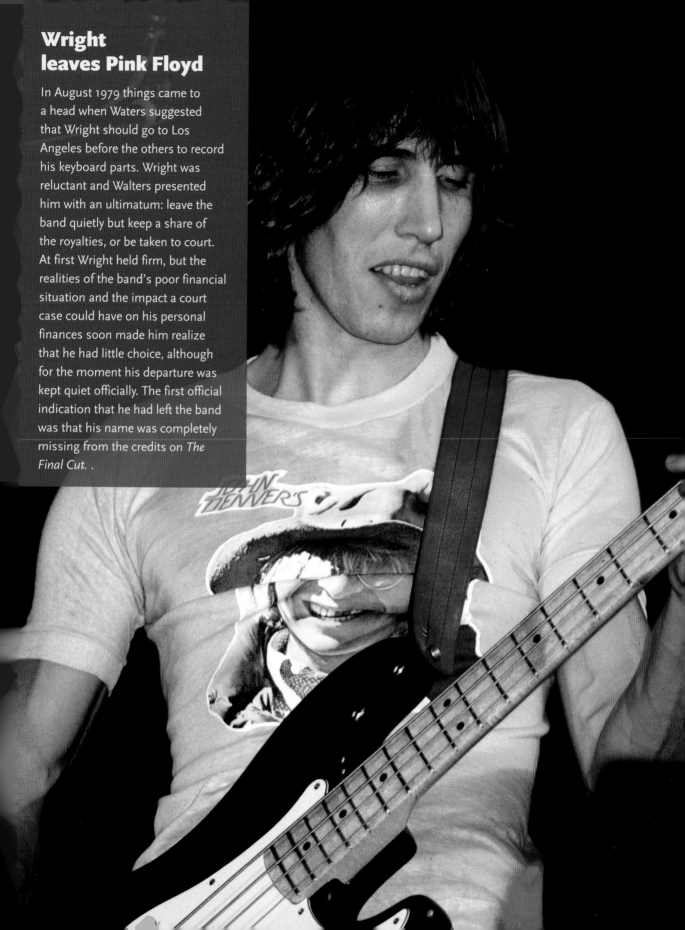

Wright leaves Pink Floyd

In August 1979 things came to a head when Waters suggested that Wright should go to Los Angeles before the others to record his keyboard parts. Wright was reluctant and Walters presented him with an ultimatum: leave the band quietly but keep a share of the royalties, or be taken to court. At first Wright held firm, but the realities of the band's poor financial situation and the impact a court case could have on his personal finances soon made him realize that he had little choice, although for the moment his departure was kept quiet officially. The first official indication that he had left the band was that his name was completely missing from the credits on *The Final Cut.* .

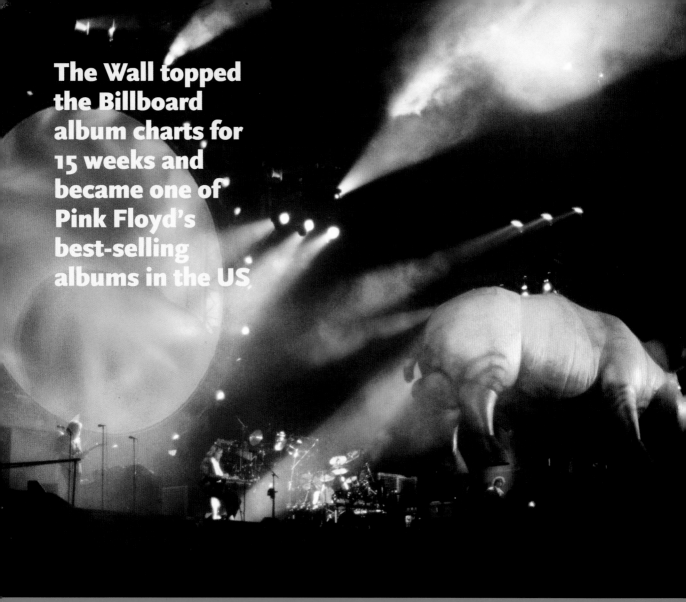

The Wall topped the Billboard album charts for 15 weeks and became one of Pink Floyd's best-selling albums in the US

The Wall — the movie

Roger Waters was the producer of the film of *The Wall* but he and the director Alan Parker often had conflicting viewpoints; their volatile relationship caused many arguments until Parker persuaded Waters to take a six-week holiday so he could work without interference. The idea was to create a movie using concert footage and animation sequences but it did not prove possible to achieve good enough results by filming the concerts themselves, so the animation segments were retained and the story was told using professional actors, with singer Bob Geldof playing the lead character, Pink.

The world première of *The Wall* movie was at the Cannes Film Festival, where it was generally well received. A few critics were critical of some of the military-style scenes, claiming that they appeared to encourage neo-Nazism, while others felt the whole movie battered the senses. Waters later said, "If I'd have directed it – which I'd never have done – it would have been much quieter than it is. He [Parker] paints in fairly bold strokes; he is very worried about boring his audience. It suits us very well, because we did want a lot of this to be a punch in the face."

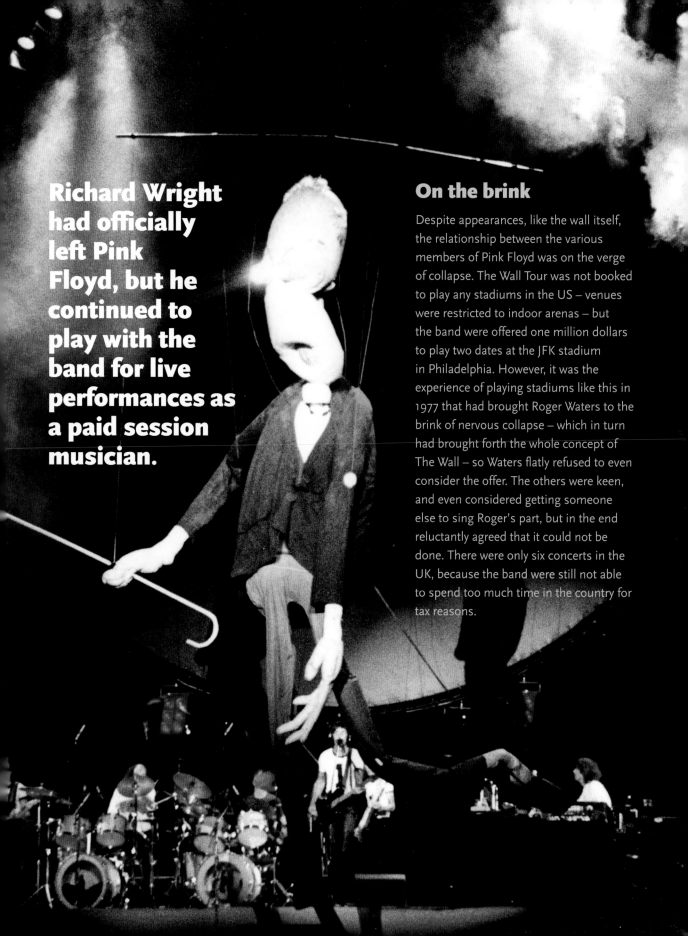

Richard Wright had officially left Pink Floyd, but he continued to play with the band for live performances as a paid session musician.

On the brink

Despite appearances, like the wall itself, the relationship between the various members of Pink Floyd was on the verge of collapse. The Wall Tour was not booked to play any stadiums in the US – venues were restricted to indoor arenas – but the band were offered one million dollars to play two dates at the JFK stadium in Philadelphia. However, it was the experience of playing stadiums like this in 1977 that had brought Roger Waters to the brink of nervous collapse – which in turn had brought forth the whole concept of The Wall – so Waters flatly refused to even consider the offer. The others were keen, and even considered getting someone else to sing Roger's part, but in the end reluctantly agreed that it could not be done. There were only six concerts in the UK, because the band were still not able to spend too much time in the country for tax reasons.

The Final Cut

Above: At Earls Court, London, 1981. The band were contracted to release a soundtrack album of *The Wall* movie, but the problem was that the movie itself had been closely based on the original *Wall* album. To resolve this, they included some unused music written for the film plus the new version of "Outside The Wall". However, Waters decided to include new tracks that he had written about the Falkland Islands conflict. In the past, all band members had a say on new material and if the majority were not convinced of its merit it would be dropped. Now the others felt that their point of view – and the spirit of compromise within the group that had been so important in the past – was being ignored, and they were not about to accept this lightly, particularly David Gilmour.

David Gilmour eventually agreed to perform on the new tracks but insisted that his name be taken off the production credits. Nick Mason had also distanced himself from the problems within the band, since he was in the midst of dealing with problems in his marriage. This effectively allowed Roger Waters a free hand, with the other members of the band just performing whatever they were given. Waters may have believed that this meant they had capitulated totally, but he was soon to realize that this was not the case. The album, *The Final Cut*, reached the No.1 spot in the UK, but sold poorly in the US and worldwide and reviews were mixed. The album's relatively poor performance confirmed to Gilmour that he was right to dislike much of its material.

Solo efforts

Right: David Gilmour was the only member of Pink Floyd to appear at Live Aid, playing guitar as part of Bryan Ferry's band and in the "Do They Know It's Christmas?" finale.

For the first time in their career Pink Floyd decided that they would not tour the *The Final Cut*, and there was also no new album in development, which left the remainder of 1983, 1984 and much of 1985 free. However, each of the three official band members, as well as Richard Wright, produced their own albums during this period – either solo or in collaboration with other musicians. David Gilmour began working at Super Bear Studios in France on *About Face*, which included performances from other musicians he admired. The album was released in 1984, and Gilmour had embarked on an extensive solo tour to promote it. Meanwhile, Roger Waters recorded on first solo album, *The Pros And Cons Of Hitch Hiking*, which was based on his alternative suggestion for Pink Floyd's 1979 album. Following its release in 1984 Waters began an extensive tour to promote it. Drummer Nick Mason began what was to become a long-term collaboration with ex-10cc guitarist Rick Fenn, which began with the pair recording a joint album, *Profiles*, which was released in 1985.

Waters quits

In late 1985, after he returned from his solo US tour, Roger Waters decided that Pink Floyd was a "spent force creatively" and he told EMI and CBS Records that he no longer wished to record as Pink Floyd. David Gilmour did not feel it was Waters' decision to terminate the band without any discussion – after all Gilmour had been a part of Pink Floyd for nearly 17 years and Mason for 20 years. It was pointed out to Waters that if he prevented the others from fulfilling their contracts he would be laying all three band members open to law suits and could be held responsible for everyone's legal expenses. As a result Waters decided to resign from Pink Floyd.

When Waters discovered that Gilmour and Mason had opened a new bank account and begun planning a new Pink Floyd album he had made an application to the High Court to prevent the Pink Floyd name being used. His case was based on the fact that Pink Floyd had originally consisted of Syd Barrett, Richard Wright, himself, and Nick Mason; his view was that now the first three founding members had left, it was not reasonable for Mason and Gilmour to continue as Pink Floyd. He also believed that since he had written most of the lyrics and much of the music for the band since Syd Barrett had left, essentially he was "Pink Floyd". The legal battles and sniping in the press became quite vicious but Waters eventually withdrew his legal action.

A Momentary Lapse of Reason

After Roger Waters left, the new set-up consisted of David Gilmour and Nick Mason, since Richard Wright could not rejoin the group officially until legal complications had been resolved. Gilmour and Mason began working on the new album in late 1986, based on material that Gilmour had already collected. One obstacle was that Waters had usually provided most of the lyrics. Several other writers were tried out to help but in the end most of the songs on the album were credited to Gilmour alone, with a few co-written by others inlcuding Anthony Moore and Bob Ezrin.

On September 7, 1987, *A Momentary Lapse of Reason* was released. Gilmour believed that it marked a return to the Floyd of older days – when the lyrics and music had equal emphasis. In an interview at the time he said, "*The Dark Side of the Moon* and *Wish You Were Here* were so successful not just because of Roger's contributions, but also because there was a better balance between the music and the lyrics." The fans seemed to agree; the album went straight to No.3 in both the UK and the US and had soon sold significantly better than *The Final Cut*. The A Momentary Lapse of Reason Tour kicked off with a concert in Ontario and was a massive success, continually breaking box office records for ticket sales across the US. As it turned out, Waters was touring the US at much the same time as his former band mates, taking his Radio Kaos tour to the kind of smaller venues he preferred.

Below: David Gilmour, Rick Wright and Nick Mason.

The Division Bell

Work began on tracks for a new Floyd album, *The Division Bell*, in early 1993. By this time both Richard Wright and Nick Mason were fully back on form and the band had hit its stride so the album was a resounding success, becoming one of the band's most successful albums to date. Its theme was the problem of communication – both personal communication between friends or lovers, and global communication between rival factions.

The Division Bell Tour featured a mixture of Floyd material from across the years, with different play lists at different venues – the entire *The Dark Side of the Moon* was played at some concerts, while others featured individual songs not necessarily in any set order. The concerts featured the usual large stage, circular screen, incredible special effects, quadrophonic sound and powerful lasers – and to keep the tour moving, three stages leapfrogged around North America and Europe, each 180 feet long and featuring a 130 foot arch modelled on the Hollywood Bowl.

The Division Bell turned out to be Pink Floyd's final studio album, although in 1995 they released a live album, *P*U*L*S*E*, which featured songs recorded during concerts in the UK and Europe during The Division Bell Tour, including a complete performance of *The Dark Side of the Moon* as well as selections from *The Wall* and *Wish You Were Here*.

At the end of 1987 agreement was reached as to how business affairs would be handled. Mason and Gilmour were allowed to continue to use the Pink Floyd name, while Waters was granted rights to The Wall and to the use of the "flying pig" image, among other things.

Together at Live 8

David Gilmour, Roger Waters, Nick Mason and Richard Wright are reunited for a performance at Live 8 London in London's Hyde Park on July 2, 2005, the first time the four had been on stage together for 24 years. Although the reunion had been orchestrated by Bob Geldof, Nick Mason later said, "You can't carry on World War Three forever. If we hadn't reformed for Live 8, we'd have done it for another charity event, I suspect." In the opinion of many critics, they went on to turn in one of their best-ever performances at the event, which apart from the live UK audience was also broadcast to millions of other Floyd fans across the world. A whole generation of younger music lovers was also introduced to Floyd music for the first time, and went on to become confirmed fans, although both Gilmour and Waters ruled out any idea of playing another tour together. Gilmour later said that Pink Floyd was over, and that Live 8 was just a good way to achieve closure.

The event was to be the last performance of the four as on September 15, 2008, Richard Wright died of cancer at his home in the UK. David Gilmour said in a tribute: "He was gentle, unassuming and private but his soulful voice and playing were vital, magical components of our most recognized Pink Floyd sound." And Roger Waters agreed, "... it is hard to overstate the importance of his musical voice in the Pink Floyd of the '60s and '70s ... Rick's ear for harmonic progression was our bedrock."

Pink Floyd took to the stage around 11.00 pm and performed four songs including "Comfortably Numb", with Gilmour and Waters sharing lead vocals.

This is a Transatlantic Press Book
First published in 2012

Transatlantic Press
38 Copthorne Road, Croxley Green, Hertfordshire, UK

© Atlantic Publishing

Photographs © Getty Images except those on pages 12 and 13

All rights reserved.
No part of this publication may be reproduced or transmitted in any form or by any means,
electronic or mechanical, including photocopying, recording, or any information storage and
retrieval system, without permission in writing from the copyright holders.

A catalogue record for this book is available from the British Library.

ISBN 978-1-908849-00-7

Printed in China